My Great Big BIRTHDAY BASH!

Betty G. Birney worked at Disneyland and the Disney Studios, has written many children's television shows and is the author of over twenty-five books, including the bestselling *The World According to Humphrey*, which won the Richard and Judy Children's Book Club Award, *Friendship According to Humphrey*, *Trouble According to Humphrey*, *Surprises According to Humphrey*, *More Adventures According to Humphrey*, *School According to Humphrey*, *Holidays According to Humphrey* and *Mysteries According to Humphrey*. Her work has won many awards, including an Emmy and three Humanitas Prizes.

her hu~b~~d~

Humphrey's Tiny Tales

My Great Big BIRTHDAY BASH!

BETTY G. BIRNEY

Illustrated by Penny Dann

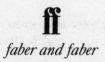

faber and faber

First published in 2012
by Faber and Faber Limited
Bloomsbury House,
74–77 Great Russell Street,
London WC1B 3DA

Printed and bound by CPI Group (UK) Ltd, Croydon, CR0 4YY

A CIP record for this book
is available from the British Library

ISBN 978–0–571–27441–3

2 4 6 8 10 9 7 5 3 1

Welcome to
MY WORLD

Hi! I'm Humphrey. I'm lucky to be
the classroom hamster in Room 26
of Longfellow School. It's a big job
because I have to go home with a
different student each weekend and
try to help my friends. Luckily, my
cage has a lock-that-doesn't-lock,
so I can get out and have
BIG-BIG-BIG adventures!

I'd like you to meet some of my friends

Og

a frog, is the other classroom pet in Room 26. He makes a funny sound: BOING!

Mrs Brisbane

is our teacher. She really understands her students – even me!

Lower-Your-Voice-A.J.

has a loud voice and calls me Humphrey Dumpty.

Raise-Your-Hand-Heidi

is always quick with an answer.

Stop-Giggling-Gail

loves to giggle – and so do I!

Repeat-It-Please-Richie

is the caretaker Aldo's nephew and a classmate of mine.

Don't-Complain-Mandy

has a hamster named Winky!

I-Heard-That-Kirk

LOVES-LOVES-LOVES to joke and have fun.

I think you'll like my other friends, too, such as *Wait-For-The-Bell-Garth*, *Golden-Miranda*, *Sit-Still-Seth* and *Speak-Up-Sayeh*.

CONTENTS

BIRTHDAYS-BIRTHDAYS-BIRTHDAYS

There are lots of exciting things that happen in Room 26 of Longfellow School.

I see them all because I live there. I am the classroom hamster.

But I think the best part of the day is when my friends come bursting through the door in the morning.

'Hi, Humphrey Dumpty!' A.J. always shouts.

A.J. has a LOUD-LOUD-LOUD voice, so I call him Lower-Your-Voice-A.J.

'Hi, A.J.!' I squeak back.

Garth is usually with A.J. because they're best friends.

I call him Wait-For-The-Bell-
Garth because he's always out of the
door first at the end of the school
day.

Then one morning, I-Heard-That-
Kirk-Chen came into our classroom
and said, 'Happy birthday to me!'

'It's
not your
birthday,
Kirk,' Mandy
said.

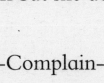

Mandy
Payne is a nice girl but she does like
to complain.

I call her Don't-Complain-
Mandy-Payne.

'It's *almost* my birthday,' Kirk said. 'It will be on Friday.'

Mandy looked up at the row of cupcakes above the chalkboard. She shook her head.

Sometimes when I look at those cupcakes, my tail twitches and my whiskers wiggle.

They look so YUMMY-YUMMY-YUMMY!

The problem is they're not real cupcakes.

They're just pictures of cupcakes with candles on top.

Each one has a name and a date.

The cupcakes help us remember when a classmate has a birthday.

One thing I've learned
from humans – birthdays are
unsqueakably important!

'No, it's not!' I heard Mandy insist
loudly.

Our teacher, Mrs Brisbane, asked,
'What's the problem?'

'Kirk says it's his birthday on
Friday, but it's not.' Mandy pointed
to the cupcakes. 'See? His birthday is
on Saturday.'

Mrs Brisbane nodded. 'Yes. But
since we don't have school on

Saturday, we're celebrating Kirk's birthday on Friday.'

'Fine,' Mandy said. 'But he shouldn't say it's his birthday when it's not.'

'Please Don't-Complain-Mandy-Payne,' Mrs Brisbane said.

'Hey, Mandy, I've got a joke for you,' Kirk said.

He *loves* to tell jokes and I think he wanted to make Mandy smile.

'What do you give a 900-pound gorilla for his birthday?' he asked.

'I don't know,' she answered.

'Anything he wants!' Kirk said, howling with laughter.

Some of my other friends laughed,

too, like Stop-Giggling-Gail, who is always laughing.

'Anything he wants!' Repeat-It-Please-Richie said.

Richie, A.J. and Garth beat their chests and made grunting sounds.

I think they were pretending to be gorillas.

Just then, the bell rang.

School was starting and my friends all sat down.

After Mrs Brisbane took the register, Kirk raised his hand.

'Mrs Brisbane, am I going to be able to take Humphrey home for the weekend like you said?' he asked.

I live in Room 26, but I'm LUCKY-LUCKY-LUCKY that I get to go home with my friends on weekends.

Our teacher nodded. 'Yes, Kirk.'

'Good,' Kirk said. 'He'll be there for my birthday *hsab*. Everyone in class is invited.'

Hsab? What was that strange word?

The way he said it sounded like 'huh–sab'.

Mrs Brisbane looked puzzled.

'I'm glad everyone is invited,' she said. 'But I've never heard of a *hsab* before. What does it mean?'

'I can't tell you!' Kirk grinned broadly. 'H-S-A-B. You have to work it out for yourselves. That's part of the fun.'

Mrs Brisbane wrote the strange word on the board in big letters:

'Maybe if we look at the word, it will help,' she said.

Then she began teaching the class about numbers.

She said something about Jonny having twelve apples and Suzy taking away eight.

I don't know Suzy, but I hope she asked Jonny before she took away his apples!

I tried to pay attention to what Mrs Brisbane was saying, but my mind kept wandering to the word on the board.

Hsab. What on earth could it mean?

Later that night, I asked the other classroom pet, Og the frog, if he'd worked it out.

Og lives in a tank next to my cage on a table by the window.

'BOING-BOING-BOING!' he replied.

He makes a funny sound, but he's really very nice for a frog.

'Me neither,' I said.

I took out the little notebook and

pencil that I keep hidden behind the mirror in my cage.

I wrote down the word so I could take a closer look.

H-S-A-B.

I turned the notebook upside down.

I turned it sideways.

I even turned the notebook backwards.

I couldn't see the word any more.

But I could see the mirror.

In the mirror, everything looks backwards, including words.

This word looked STRANGE-STRANGE-STRANGE.

I saw a backwards B, an A, a backwards S and an H.

If the backwards letters were

forwards, the word would be

B-A-S-H!

A bash! A bash is like a great, big wonderful party.

So Kirk was having a birthday bash!

But why did he write the word backwards?

Humans are nice, but sometimes they do very strange things.

I wasn't the only one in Room 26 who had worked out that *hsab* was bash spelled backwards.

'It's a birthday bash,' A.J. shouted as he came into class the next morning. 'I got the invitation and my mum held it up to the mirror. Some of the letters were backwards, but she worked it out.'

A.J.'s mum must be SMART-SMART-SMART (like me).

Mrs Brisbane asked Kirk to explain why he had written the word backwards.

'It's a backwards party,'
he said. 'Everything will be
backwards. Hands up if you're
coming.'

Every hand in the room shot
up.

My paw went up, too.

'It sounds like a very interesting party,' Mrs Brisbane said.

'Mrs Brisbane?' Mandy said. 'I've been looking at the birthday cupcakes and some names are missing.'

Our teacher looked up at the row of cupcakes.

'Yours isn't up there,' Mandy continued. 'Or Humphrey's.'

I scrambled up to the tippy-top of my cage to see if she was right.

Sure enough, Mrs Brisbane's name wasn't there and neither was mine.

Another name was also missing.

'What about Og?' I squeaked at the top of my tiny lungs.

'Ooh, Og's missing, too,' Raise-Your-Hand-Heidi said.

As usual, she forgot to raise her hand.

When I squeak, humans can't understand me, so I was glad that Heidi had also noticed that Og's name was missing.

'I don't need everyone to remember my birthday,' Mrs Brisbane said. 'Every day I'm here in Room 26 is a special day for me.'

My friends still wanted to know about Og and me.

'The problem is, I don't know when they were born,' Mrs Brisbane said.

I suddenly felt
SAD–SAD–SAD.

If no one knew
when I was born, I
could never have a
birthday!

Heidi said, 'Frogs aren't born.
They're hatched!'

'That's right,' Mrs Brisbane said.
'Frogs start out as eggs.'

Og splashed around a little in his
tank.

I felt SAD–SAD–SAD for him, too.

He could never have a birthday.

And though he could have a
hatch-day, nobody knew when it
was.

A SILLY-SILLY-SILLY
Party

On Friday, we celebrated Kirk's
birthday in class.

First, he got to wear the paper
birthday crown all day.

Next, he got to pick a gift from
Mrs Brisbane's birthday grab bag.

She asked him to close his eyes and
reach inside.

The birthday surprise he pulled out was a big sheet of silly stickers.

I was glad it was something funny, since Kirk likes to joke around.

Then we all sang him a birthday song.

I happily squeaked along and I even heard a few BOING-BOINGS coming from Og.

At the end of the day, Kirk's mum came to pick us up.

'Bye, Og,' I squeaked. 'I'll tell you all about the bash on Monday.'

Og doesn't leave Room 26 at the weekends, because he can go a few days without being fed.

I didn't like leaving him behind.

He didn't have his own hatch-day *and* he wasn't going to Kirk's birthday bash.

I guess it's not easy being a frog.

The next day, when it was time for the party, Kirk set me on a big table near the front door so I could see everything.

'Just watch, Humphrey,' he said. 'The fun is about to begin.'

And something funny had already begun because Kirk had his shirt on back to front so the buttons went down his back!

Most of his clothes were on back to front, except his shoes.

I think it would be hard for a human to walk in back-to-front shoes.

The doorbell rang and Kirk ran to open it.

'Goodbye,' he said as Richie entered.

Kirk turned Richie around and said, 'Not like that! You have to come in backwards.'

So Richie came through the door again, walking backwards.

He wasn't just walking backwards.

He was also wearing his clothes inside out!

Because it was a backwards party, all my friends from Room 26 arrived wearing their clothes back to front or inside out.

Everyone loved the birthday balloons, which were attached to the floor instead of the ceiling.

And they laughed at the music, which sounded STRANGE-STRANGE-STRANGE because it was playing backwards.

Then my friends had a relay race in the garden.

It was unsqueakably funny to see them running backwards.

My friends laughed, too.

One nice thing about humans is that they can laugh at themselves.

At last, it was time to eat.

Kirk moved my cage to a little table near the big table where all my friends were gathered.

Kirk's mum brought in the birthday cake.

On top, were bright red icing letters: KRIK, YADHTRIB YPPAH.

I had a pretty good idea that those letters spelled out: HAPPY BIRTHDAY, KIRK – only backwards!

Singing the birthday song backwards wasn't easy but Kirk's

dad had printed out the words so everyone could take part.

Then, instead of blowing out his birthday candles, Kirk helped his mum light them.

'Make a wish,' Kirk's mum said.

Kirk closed his eyes and opened them again.

Then he blew out the candles.

But the funny thing was, they lit right up again!

Kirk tried to blow them out again and again, but they kept relighting because they were trick candles.

'Backwards candles,' Kirk said. 'Funny!'

Finally, Kirk's dad put them out.

Then, Kirk's mum served ice cream.

'Hey, what did the ice cream say to the cake?' Kirk asked.

No one answered, so Kirk said, 'What's eating you?'

I laughed and laughed – it was such a funny joke!

Kirk's friends gave him presents wrapped in inside-out paper with bows tied on the bottom instead of the top.

He got a toy helicopter, some rocks for his rock collection, a board game and a joke book.

I think the joke book was his favourite present because he started reading it right away.

'Hey, what does a cat eat for his birthday?' he asked. '*Mice* cream and cake!'

Everybody laughed except me.

After all, mice and hamsters are a lot alike.

I was SO-SO-SO embarrassed that I didn't have a present for Kirk.

But then I had an idea.

I may not have had a present, but at least I could add something to the party.

I decided to put on a show.

First, I started spinning on my wheel.

The sound got Richie's attention.

'Hey, look at Humphrey go!' he said.

Soon, all my friends were gathered around my cage, watching.

I hopped off my wheel and climbed up the big tree branch in my cage, all the way to the top.

'Oooh,' my friends said.

Then I grabbed on to the top bars and hung on tightly.

Slowly and carefully, I made my way across the top of the cage.

'Ahhh!' my friends said.

To finish off the act, I made a daring jump straight down and landed in my bedding.

I hadn't planned to do a double-flip, but when I did, my

friends all clapped.

When it was time for the guests to leave, everyone said 'Hello,' which made me giggle.

'Hello!' I squeaked loudly.

After everyone had gone home, Kirk said, 'Thank you, Humphrey, for helping make my party turn out so well!'

'Thanks for inviting me,' I squeaked back.

I don't think I'd ever had so much fun in my life.

I only wished Og could have been there, too.

When I got back to Room 26 on Monday morning, I was about to tell my froggy friend about the backwards bash when I heard Garth say, 'Listen up, everybody.'

He looked over at my cage.

Then he glanced at the door, where Mrs Brisbane was talking to the teacher across the hall.

'I have a great idea. Want to hear

it?' Garth asked in a loud whisper.

'Yes!' the other students yelled.

'YES-YES-YES!' I squeaked.

'Sssh,' he said. 'It's a secret. Listen up.'

Garth turned to Richie and whispered something in his ear.

All I could hear were the words '*surprise*' and '*Thursday*'.

I like surprises and wanted to hear more.

'Could you squeak up just a little?' I asked.

Richie turned to Miranda and whispered in her ear.

I perked up my tiny pink ears but all I could hear was the word '*present*'.

Miranda smiled. 'Oooh, I have an idea!'

'Sssh,' the other children told her.

'Sorry,' Miranda said.

Then Miranda turned to Gail and whispered in her ear.

Gail giggled, then whispered in A.J.'s ear.

This time, I heard the word 'birthday'.

Next, A.J. whispered in Kirk's ear.

A.J.'s voice is so loud, even when he whispers, A.J. is loud.

I couldn't hear everything he said but I did hear him say 'Mrs Brisbane'.

So that was the secret!

They were having a surprise birthday party for Mrs Brisbane on Thursday!

My whiskers wiggled at the exciting news.

But I wished my friends had whispered in my ear, too, so I'd know more about the plans.

Mrs Brisbane came over to the group.

'Why are you all whispering?' she asked.

'It's a secret,' A.J. said.

Mrs Brisbane smiled. 'As long as it's a good secret, I guess that's okay.'

She glanced over at my cage and said, 'Isn't that right, Humphrey?'

I wasn't sure if secrets were ever okay.

Before I could answer, the bell rang and Mrs Brisbane started class.

I always try to listen to every word she says.

But it wasn't easy to listen when my mind was racing with thoughts about Mrs Brisbane's surprise birthday party.

Would it be backwards or forwards?

Would there be games?

And most importantly, would there be cake?

Cake is *unsqueakably* important at a birthday party.

A GREAT-GREAT-GREAT
Escape

The next few days I was pawsitively
happy all the time.

I'd watch Mrs Brisbane teaching
and think about how happy she'd be
on Thursday when the whole class
shouted, 'Surprise!'

I'd hear my friends whispering
about 'presents' and I'd think about

how she'd smile when she opened her gifts.

I even practised the birthday song in my mirror.

This time, I squeaked it forwards, not backwards.

I *was* puzzled by a few things that happened during the week.

On Tuesday, Sayeh and Seth suddenly started measuring my cage with a ruler.

They also measured Og's tank.

'It's for a maths problem,' Sayeh said.

Sometimes, Mrs Brisbane has students measure things for maths, so that made sense.

On Wednesday, when my friends worked on an art project, Mandy raised her hand and asked how to spell my name.

Mrs Brisbane wrote, 'Humphrey' on the board.

She also let the students work a lot longer than usual on their art.

Even though hamsters like me are often awake at night, on Wednesday night, I thought I should get some sleep.

After all, I wanted to be wide awake for Mrs Brisbane's surprise birthday party the next day.

I dozed for a while and I had a very strange dream.

First I dreamed about YUMMY-YUMMY-YUMMY dancing cupcakes.

Then I dreamed about the look on Mrs Brisbane's face when she saw her gifts and cake and we all squeaked 'Happy Birthday' to her.

Suddenly I woke up with a terrible thought.

'Og!' I squeaked. 'We forgot something.'

Og splashed around in his tank.

I jiggled the lock on my cage door.

It seemed tightly locked, but I have a secret way to open it.

That's why I call it the lock-that-doesn't-lock.

I jiggled the lock some more.

When it opened, I was free!

I hurried across the table to Og's tank.

'Og, we forgot to get a present for Mrs Brisbane!' I told him. 'Just like I forgot to get one for Kirk!'

'BOING-BOING-BOING!' he answered excitedly.

'We have to give her something so she'll know we're glad she's our teacher,' I explained. 'But what?'

Og stared at me from his tank, but he didn't answer.

I guessed it was up to me to think of an idea.

We couldn't go to the shops to buy something, so we'd have to make her a gift.

I looked up at the chalkboard, with the row of cupcakes around it.

'I know,' I said. 'Let's make her a cake. After all, you can't have too much cake at a birthday party!'

'BOING-BOING-BOING!' Og hopped up and down.

'Of course, we can't *bake* a cake,' I said. 'But we can make her a hamster-and-frog kind of cake.'

'BOING!' Og agreed.

I went back into my cage and was delighted to see that my food dish was full of crunchy Nutri-Nibbles.

It's one of my favourite treats.

One by one, I put a few Nutri-Nibbles in my cheek pouch, carried them out of the cage, and set them down in front of Og's tank.

After a while I had a nice stack of them.

Nutri-Nibbles are a little too crunchy to make a cake.

'I need your help, Og,' I said.

'BOING-BOING!' he answered.

'Splash a lot of water so it goes on the Nutri-Nibbles,' I said.

Then I scampered out of the way, because water isn't good for hamsters.

Og splashed . . . and splashed some more.

His tank has a top, but if he splashes hard enough, some of the water spills out of the crack at the top.

Soon, the pile of Nutri-Nibbles was nice and wet.

'Thanks, Og,' I said.

Then I went straight to work, using my paws to pat and smooth the Nutri-Nibbles batter into a circle.

'It *looks* like a cake,' I said. 'But it's awfully plain.'

'BOING-BOING,' Og agreed.

So I went back into the cage and dug around in my bedding, where

sometimes I store food.

I found two strawberries and three raisins and pressed them into the side of the cake.

Next, I scurried to the back of the table where Mrs Brisbane keeps food and supplies for Og and me.

There were big bags of Mighty Mealworms, Healthy Dots, Nutri-Nibbles, Hamster Chew-Chews and nice soft hay. Yum!

There was also a box of Og's Froggy Fish Sticks and a can of crickets!

Yep, that's what frogs eat. Eww!

I chewed a small hole in the bag of hay and made several trips back and forth to the cake.

Soon it had a nice frosting of soft hay on top.

Then I added a Chew-Chew, which almost looked like a candle.

'BOING-BOING-BOING!' Og said. 'BOING-BOING-BOING-*BOING*!'

I thought the cake looked great, but Og seemed a little *too* excited about it.

'Just one more thing,' I told him. 'I think a few Healthy Dots would look nice.'

Healthy Dots are good for hamsters, but they also come in lots of colours and look like sweets.

Og splashed crazily in his tank, but I scurried to the back of the table once again.

I was trying to work out how to open the box when I heard people talking.

'BOING-BOING-*BOING*!' Og twanged.

I couldn't see anything, but when
I heard A.J.'s loud voice, I knew my
friends had come into the classroom.

I looked up at the window.

It was already light outside!

I heard Mrs Brisbane saying, 'Good
morning.'

I heard the bell ring, too.

The school day was starting!

It was the first time I wasn't in my
cage when my friends were in the
room.

I was STUCK-STUCK-STUCK.

A BIG-BIG-BIG Surprise

Mrs Brisbane took the register.

Then I heard Heidi say, 'Can we do it now?'

Heidi sounded unsqueakably excited.

'I think we should wait until just before break,' Mrs Brisbane said.

I could hear more talking, but I

couldn't understand it all.

I can hear fine in my cage, but from my hiding place behind Healthy Dots, the sounds were muffled.

If only I could see what was going on!

I thought I heard Garth ask, 'Where's Humphrey? I don't see him.'

Then Mrs Brisbane said something about me making a map.

Or maybe she said I was taking a nap.

I would have been so happy to be taking a nap instead of being stuck outside my cage.

I wasn't exactly sure what would happen next.

Maybe my friends would discover I was missing and find out about the lock-that-doesn't-lock.

If they fixed it, I'd be trapped in my cage for ever!

Or, maybe no one would notice I

wasn't in my cage and I'd miss out
on Mrs Brisbane's birthday party!

I didn't like either of those ideas
one bit.

Og splashed nervously in his tank.

I crossed my toes and hoped that
everyone would leave the classroom
so I could return to my cage.

Or at least that my friends would

get so busy they wouldn't notice me sneaking back.

Then I heard Mrs Brisbane say, 'It's time.'

Which was odd, because the birthday party was supposed to be a surprise for her.

Next, I heard lots of whispering and rustling.

I heard footsteps moving closer and closer.

I heard Gail giggle and someone said, 'Sssh!'

Then Mrs Brisbane whispered, 'Ready?'

Suddenly, all of my classmates screamed, 'SURPRISE!'

'Come on out, Humphrey Dumpty,' A.J. shouted. 'It's time for your birthday party!'

Sayeh's softer voice said, 'And Og's hatch-day party.'

'BOING!' Og said.

My birthday party? Og's hatch-day party?

I was amazed.

The surprise party wasn't for Mrs Brisbane.

The surprise party was for Og and me.

But the biggest surprise was the fact that I was missing my own celebration!

'Where is he?' Richie asked.

Og splashed wildly.

I think he was as confused as I was.

'Come on out, Humphrey. We want to wish you Happy Birthday,' Mrs Brisbane said.

I didn't know what to do, so I sat and waited.

Then Mrs Brisbane told someone to open the cage and a few seconds later, I heard Garth say, 'He's not here!'

Of course, everyone thought that was impossible.

There were more rustling noises.

'You're right,' Mrs Brisbane said. 'I don't think Humphrey's in his cage. I wonder if someone left the door unlocked. Or maybe it's broken.'

I heard the cage door open and shut a few times.

'No, Mrs Brisbane,' Art said. 'It works just fine.'

'We must all look for him,' Mrs Brisbane said. 'But we'll have to be very careful not to step on him.'

'Eeek!' I squeaked.

I didn't mean to say it, but just thinking of someone stepping on me, it came out.

'I can hear him!' Miranda said.

Oops!

There was no hiding now, so I decided it was time to show myself.

'Surprise!' I squeaked as I scurried across the table.

'There's Humphrey Dumpty!' A.J. shouted.

Mrs Brisbane scooped me up and put me back in my cage.

'Humphrey, when your friends told me they wanted to give you a surprise party, I never dreamed you wouldn't show up for it,' she said.

So, Mrs Brisbane was in on it all along!

'I don't know how you got out, but please don't do it again,' she said to me.

I didn't squeak back to her, but I was pretty sure I *would* get out of my cage again.

Only next time, I wouldn't get caught!

After that, I had an unsqueakably wonderful time!

Sayeh put a paper birthday crown on top of my cage.

Richie put a paper birthday crown on top of Og's tank.

Then they put a big banner across
my cage, which said, 'HAPPY
BIRTHDAY HUMPHREY!'

So *that's* why they measured my
cage.

Another banner went across Og's
tank.

It said, 'HAPPY HATCH-DAY OG!'

They gave us cards.

That was their art project.

And they gave us presents.

Og got a special rock that he could climb over or hide under.

And I got something amazing – a tiny bell that makes an unsqueakably nice tinkling sound when I touch it.

It was the BEST-BEST-BEST
present I could imagine!

But my ears
perked up when
I heard A.J.'s loud
voice say, 'Cake
time!'

'It looks as
if Humphrey
already has one,' Mrs Brisbane said,
leaning down to look at the tiny cake
I had made.

'Who made this cute little cake?'
she asked.

No one answered, so I decided to
squeak up.

'I did,' I said. 'I made it for you.'

Mrs Brisbane laughed.

'I guess it's a secret,' she said. 'But Humphrey seems to know who it was.'

I DID-DID-DID!

Then I was presented with the most beautiful cake I've ever seen.

It was made of nuts and seeds and raisins – all my favourite foods!

The whole class sang the Happy
Birthday song to me.

Then they gave Og a cake made
of things he likes and sang a Happy

Hatch-day song to him.

He splashed around happily when they put it in his tank.

★ ★ ★

At the end of the day, when all my friends had left, Mrs Brisbane came over to our table.

'I hope you liked your party,' she said.

'It was unsqueakably wonderful,' I answered. 'But it was supposed to be for *you*!'

I know that all she heard was SQUEAK-SQUEAK-SQUEAK.

But Mrs Brisbane laughed and said, 'Happy Birthday, Humphrey and Og.'

I said, 'Happy Birthday, Mrs Brisbane.'

Og said, 'BOING-BOING-BOING!'

We both agreed it really was the best birthday bash ever.

I was surprised that the party was for us and not Mrs Brisbane.

And my *friends* were surprised that I wasn't around for my own party.

'I hope we have another birthday and hatch-day party next year,' I told Og when we were alone for the night.

'And I still hope we have a surprise birthday party for Mrs Brisbane,' I added.

'BOING-BOING!' he said.

And then I rang my bell a few more times, just for fun.

Have you ready all my tiny tales?

See what unsqueakably exciting adventures I've had . .

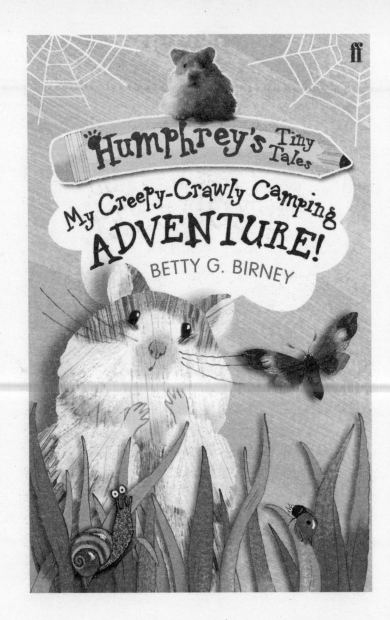

Humphrey's Tiny Tales

My Creepy-Crawly Camping ADVENTURE!

BETTY G. BIRNEY

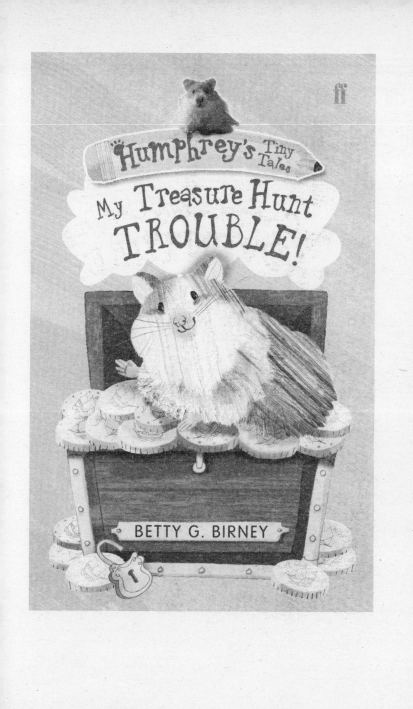

Humphrey's Tiny Tales

My Treasure Hunt
TROUBLE!

BETTY G. BIRNEY

Dear friends,

Humans love their pets, and pets like me love their humans. I'm unsqueakably excited to share everything I've learned in Classroom 26 and beyond about the world of pets with you.

And hamsters aren't the only pets! Do you know how to look after a chinchilla? What is a puppy's favourite food? As well as learning top pet-care tips, you can tell me all about your pets in the special My Precious Pet section. I can't wait to meet them!

Your furry friend,

Humphrey

PET-tastic facts

WOUF!

LOTS
of fun
inside!

Humphrey's
World of Pets

Betty G. Birney

Look for my book of
unsqueakably funny jokes

Or why not try the
puzzles and games in my
fun-fun-fun activity
book!

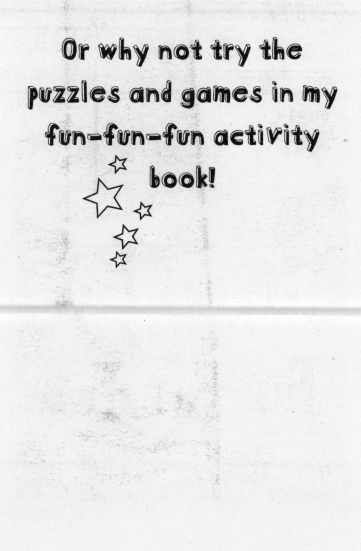

Puzzles and Games

From everybody's favourite hamster: ME!!

Secret Codes!

Jokes!

Puzzles!

Humphrey's Book of Fun-Fun-Fun

ff

Betty G. Birney

Humphrey and his friends have been
hard at work making a brand new
FUN-FUN-FUN website just for you!

Play Humphrey's exciting new game,
share your pet pictures, find fun crafts
and activities, read Humphrey's very
own diary and discover all the latest
news from your favourite furry
friend at:

www.funwithhumphrey.com